KAI
The Honu Who Didn't Know He Was Brave

Written by Mora Ebie
Illustrated by Mike Tackett

MUTUAL PUBLISHING

Created with aloha for my sister, Meredith.
You are the bravest little honu I know. Mahalo.

— Mora Ebie

ISBN-10: 1-56647-755-7
ISBN-13: 978-1-56647-755-0
Library of Congress Catalog Card Number: 2005931211

Design by Emily R. Lee

Fourteenth Printing, April 2018

Mutual Publishing, LLC
1215 Center Street, Suite 210
Honolulu, Hawai'i 96816
Ph: 808-732-1709 / Fax: 808-734-4094
Email: info@mutualpublishing.com
www.mutualpublishing.com

Printed in Taiwan

Beneath the deep blue waters of Hawai'i, a small honu named Kai swam along the green seaweed. His Hawaiian name was 'Aukai, but all the sea creatures called him Kai. Kai had a yellow body and a strong green shell. Even though Kai knew his shell was strong and sturdy, he was afraid of everything he saw.

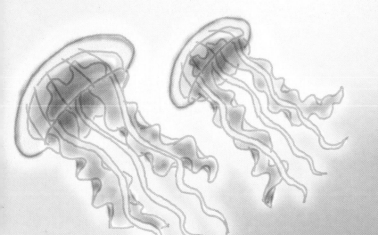

"Aloha, Kai!" a familiar voice called out. Kai turned his head and saw his friend, Polo Ka'ahele, swimming towards him.

"Aloha, Polo," Kai replied. "What are you doing?"

"Miki and I are playing hide-and-go-seek," Polo replied. "She's hiding somewhere. Can you help me find her?"

"Sure," Kai said, and he followed Polo along the bottom of the sea.

Suddenly, Kai saw a giant eel
with glowing red eyes and sharp giant teeth
swimming towards him! He ducked behind some
coral to hide from the terrifying beast. He waited for
a few minutes and when he thought it was safe,
Kai slowly emerged from his coral hiding
place. He was surprised to find Polo
waiting for him.

"Kai, Miki is the one who's supposed to be hiding!" Polo said.

"But, look! There's an eel!" Kai trembled as he pointed behind Polo.

Polo turned and laughed. "Oh, Kai. That's just the sunshine shimmering through a clump of long seaweed. Don't be so silly."

"Oh, sorry," Kai whispered,
and he swam after Polo once more.

"I think Miki is hiding down there,"
Polo said as he swam down to
where the water got darker.

"Wait!" Kai yelled as a flicker of movement caught
his eye. "There's a sea monster down there!"

Polo peered down and began to laugh.
"Kai, that's just a school of fish
swimming near a huge coral reef!"

"Oh," Kai said slowly as the fish swam by him.

Polo swam down to the coral reef and squealed with delight. "Miki! I found you!"

Miki, a quick green honu, emerged from the coral. "What took you so long?"

"Kai was helping me," Polo answered, "but he kept getting scared by imaginary monsters."

Kai suddenly felt hot and red. He was embarrassed. He didn't like being so afraid.

"Silly honu," Miki said. "Well, I guess it's my turn to find you guys. I'll count to 20, and then I'll come and find you. One . . . two . . . three . . ."

"Come on!" Polo said as he quickly swam away.

Kai was a faster swimmer than Polo, so he quickly passed his friend. As he searched for a hiding place, Kai suddenly saw a huge shark below him! He turned to swim away, when BUMP! He swam right into Polo!

"Hey! That hurt!" Polo moaned, rubbing his head.

"We've got to swim away!" Kai cried. "There's a shark down there!"

Polo looked down and began to laugh again. "Silly honu," he said. "That's not a shark. It's just a sunken boat!"

Kai turned around and looked down. Polo was right. It wasn't a shark at all, but an old boat that gently rested on the ocean floor.

"I thought the sails were fins," Kai explained, "and the wood was teeth… and…"

"Aha! I found you!" Miki yelled as she swam up to them.

"I didn't even get a chance to hide," Polo said with a frown. "Kai thought he saw a shark. It was just an old boat on the ocean floor."

"Kai!" Miki sighed. "You have to stop being so afraid!"

Miki continued to speak as a dark shadow crept from behind her.

"You're interrupting our game with your silly imaginary monsters," Miki said, as the shadow got closer and closer.

Kai's eyes got bigger and bigger as the shadow got darker behind his two friends.

"You're such a Scaredy-Honu!" Polo laughed as the shadow froze.

"Excuse me," a deep voice said from behind. The dark shadow covered Polo and Miki. They slowly turned to see a terrible sight in front of them. A huge shark!

"I don't think that's a boat!" Kai whispered.

Kai looked at his two friends. Their eyes were just as wide as his! They were scared!

"I was looking for a tasty snack," the shark said. "Do you think three little honu will fit in my tummy?"

Kai looked at his friends. They were frozen with fear. Kai knew he had to do something before the big shark ate them all! He took a deep breath and summoned up every drop of courage he had in his tiny body.

"Look! A manta ray!" Kai said, pointing past the shark.

The shark turned suddenly, looking for his favorite snack. "A manta ray? Where?"

Kai grabbed his friends and swam away as fast as he could.

"Hey!" the shark yelled, angry that he had been tricked. "Come back here!"

Kai was a very strong and quick swimmer. He darted through coral and around large rocks and along seaweed. Polo and Miki stayed right at his side. The shark took empty bites at their fins as the three friends swam away as fast as they could!

"Kai, the shark is getting closer! What are we going to do?" Miki cried.

Kai suddenly spotted a hole in the coral ahead. "Follow me!" he yelled and swam toward the hole.

Kai and his friends easily swam through the hole in the coral. But the shark was so big, he got stuck in the hole! He wriggled as hard as he could, but he was stuck!

"You did it, Kai!" Polo said as they neared the ocean shore. The three friends laid on the beach and took a heavy breath. Polo looked at Kai and said, "I was wrong, Kai. You're not a Scaredy-Honu at all. You're very brave."

"I guess I'm brave when I have to be," Kai said with a proud smile.

"You outsmarted a shark! That's very brave indeed," Miki said.

And from that day on,
Kai was known as the bravest
honu in the sea!

Mora Ebie has spent many years exploring the Islands. While studying for her graduate degree, Mora researched her thesis on Hawaiian children's literature on O'ahu and Maui. There she met many lovely teachers and keiki, whose influence led her to write stories for them. She currently lives in Los Angeles, California, where she spends her time teaching first grade, writing funny stories, planning more visits to the Islands, and spending time with her husband Chris and their two mischievous kittens, Emma and Schroeder.

Mike Tackett is a freelance illustrator, web designer, animator, and cartoonist. Having earned a Masters in Computer Science from Washington State University, he started his professional career as a software developer but was always interested in illustrating. The graphics side took over completely and though Mike still spends time on the computer, it is mostly for the purpose of creating digital art. Island flavor has permeated his drawings since he was introduced to Hawai'i and its culture and history 30 years ago—he has never been the same since.

9/13

CR

I0587159

ASTONISHING BODIES

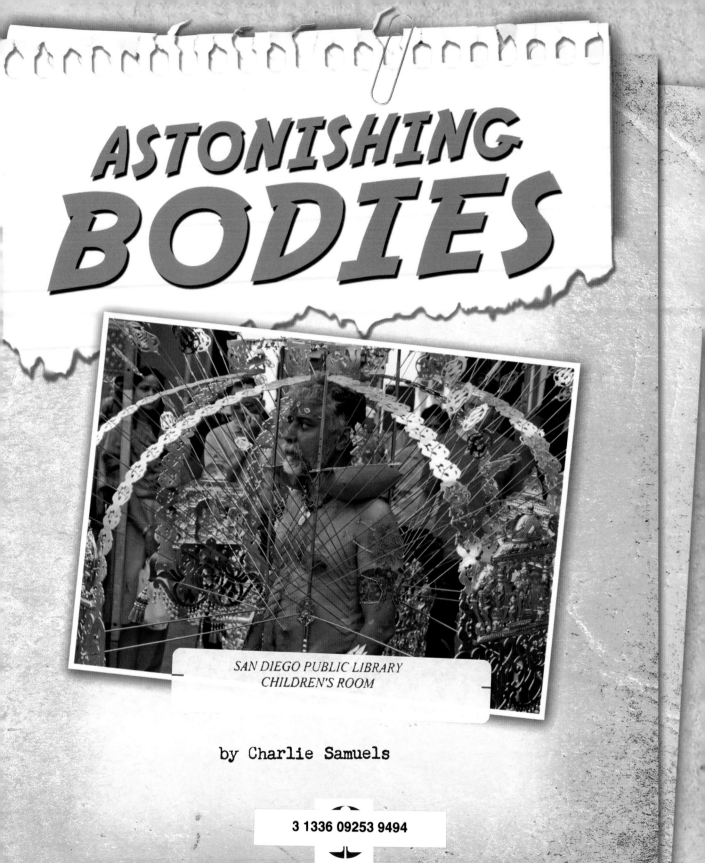

by Charlie Samuels

Crabtree Publishing Company

www.crabtreebooks.com

Crabtree Publishing Company

www.crabtreebooks.com

Author: Charlie Samuels
Project Coordinator: Kathy Middleton
Editors: Molly Aloian, Tim Cooke
Proofreader: Crystal Sikkens
Designer: Lynne Lennon
Cover Design: Margaret Amy Salter
Picture Researcher: Andrew Webb
Picture Manager: Sophie Mortimer
Art Director: Jeni Child
Editorial Director: Lindsey Lowe
Children's Publisher: Anne O'Daly
Production Coordinator and
    Prepress Technician: Samara Parent
Print Coordinator: Katherine Berti

Photographs
Cover: Wikimedia Commons: Wohlschlegelm
Interior: Alamy: Thierry Grun 15, Mary Evans Picture Library 13; **Associated Press:** 21; **istockphoto:** 14, 16 26; **Science Photo Library:** Jay Coneyl 24, Jeremy Walker 25; **Shutterstock:** 17, 19, Circlephoto 12, Everett Collection 7, Image Source 5, Teck Sion Ong 4, Tonis Pan 22, James Steidl 6; **The Kobal Collecion:** Black Owl Productions 8, MGM 18; **Thinkstock:** Comstock 11, istockphoto 28, Photos.com 29; **Topfoto:** 10, Fortean 9, PA Photos 23, RIA Novosti 20, Linda Rich/ArenaPAL 27.

Library and Archives Canada Cataloguing in Publication

Samuels, Charlie, 1961-
    Astonishing bodies / Charlie Samuels.

(Mystery files)
Includes index.
Issued also in electronic formats.
ISBN 978-0-7787-8006-9 (bound).--ISBN 978-0-7787-8011-3 (pbk.)

    1. Human body--Juvenile literature. 2. Human physiology--Juvenile
literature. I. Title. II. Series: Mystery files (St. Catharines, Ont.)

QP37.S26 2012   j612   C2012-906795-4

Library of Congress Cataloging-in-Publication Data

CIP available at Library of Congress

Crabtree Publishing Company

www.crabtreebooks.com   1-800-387-7650

Published in Canada
Crabtree Publishing
616 Welland Ave.
St. Catharines, ON
L2M 5V6

Published in the United States
Crabtree Publishing
PMB 59051
350 Fifth Avenue, 59th Floor
New York, New York 10118

Published by CRABTREE PUBLISHING COMPANY in 2013
Copyright © 2013 Brown Bear Books Ltd

Printed in the U.S.A./112012/FA20121012

Contents

Introduction   4

Superhuman STRENGTH   6

Spontaneous COMBUSTION   8

Human HIBERNATION   10

SLEEPWALKING   12

Walking on FIRE   14

Human PINCUSHIONS   16

Wild CHILDREN   18

Human MAGNETS   20

Bionic BODIES   22

Extra Sensory PERCEPTION   24

Elastic BODIES   26

Holding their BREATH   28

Glossary   30

Find Out More   31

Index   32

Introduction

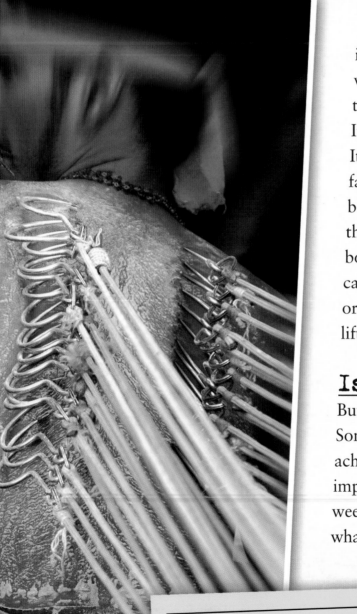

The human body is remarkable. Every day, it does many amazing things without you even knowing. It turns food and air into energy. It pumps blood to your limbs. It moves around without falling over. Most peoples' bodies cannot function beyond these limits. For example, the body does not like pain. It cannot survive extreme cold or go without air. It cannot lift huge weights.

Is That Possible?

But that is not always the case. Some people claim to have achieved **feats** that seem impossible, such as surviving for weeks in freezing temperatures. Is what they are saying even possible?

A Hindu man uses hooks in his skin to pull a heavy load.

Incredible Feats

This book examines some astonishing **oddities** of the human body. Some, such as great strength or sleepwalking, are familiar. Others, such as **spontaneous** human **combustion**, still remain mysteries to scientists. It is hard for anyone to understand why a person would burst into flames for no reason!

You'll meet children who claim to have been raised by wild animals and worshipers who show their **devotion** by piercing their skin with blades and hooks. You'll meet people who can walk on fire. You will discover just how remarkable the human body can be.

5

Superhuman
STRENGTH

In movies, superheroes can lift cars or buildings. What about humans? There are many stories of great feats of strength, such as a mother lifting an entire car to save her child trapped underneath.

People have been fascinated by the strength of the human body since ancient times. A Greek myth tells how the hero Atlas held the world on his shoulders. Ancient peoples held weightlifting competitions to test the limits of their strength. Today, scientists understand which body types are better suited for lifting weights. Shorter limbs lift more weight than long ones. Training and good nutrition help develop bigger muscles.

Mystery words...

adrenaline: a chemical in the body that helps it to overcome pain

Animal Comparisons

Today, people test their strength by pulling trucks or carrying heavy rocks. The strongest weightlifters can lift about 475 pounds (215 kilograms). Some animals are far stronger than humans in proportion to their size. For example, ants can lift up to 50 times their body weight. For a human, this would mean lifting well over 1,100 pounds (500 kg).

Mystery File: MIRACLE STRENGTH

How do ordinary people find superhuman strength in an emergency? **Adrenaline** gives them a burst of hysterical strength. Hysterical strength allows them to lift cars or push down walls to save themselves or their loved ones.

Spontaneous COMBUSTION

Can a person suddenly burst into flames? Cases of spontaneous human combustion have been reported since the 17th century. But many scientists doubt that the phenomenon really exists.

Spontaneous human combustion occurs in many movies.

According to accounts, spontaneous human combustion happens without warning. A person's torso and head are suddenly **engulfed** in flames. The victim usually burns to death. The legs and feet are often left unburned. The idea that spontaneous human combustion can happen became widespread after the author Charles Dickens described it in his novel *Bleak House* in 1852.

Mystery words...

engulfed: completely covered

Not So Spontaneous

People who believe in spontaneous combustion suggest that gas in the stomach generates heat that bursts into flames. The fire burns fat in the body, which acts like the wick of a candle. Others say that such fires are not spontaneous. A spark must have set light to the victim. The wick-effect causes body fat to burn. The flames burn upward, which is why the legs and feet are often unharmed.

In 2004, a dead sperm whale combusted as it was being transported to a laboratory in Taiwan. It caught fire because methane-producing bacteria had built up in its stomach. The explosion showered the local area with whale meat.

Police clean up after a woman is said to have combusted in Florida in 1951.

Human
HIBERNATION

Some humans have survived long periods of freezing cold. Others have been buried but still managed to survive. Is it possible for people to shut down the normal functions of their bodies, like animals that hibernate during the winter?

Animals such as bears hibernate to conserve energy. Their heart rate slows right down. They also need less oxygen and food. They can spend months in this semiconscious state.

Yogis are deeply religious men from India. They meditate by training their minds to go into a **trance**. During their trances, they claim to be able to go without much food or water, and even with little air.

Yogis claim to be able to survive a temporary burial.

10

In the 1970s, scientists tested Yogi Satyamurti. He spent eight days in a deep state of **meditation**. His heart rate fell so low, he should have died. But when he came out of the trance, he was in great shape.

Surviving the Cold

There are many reports of skiers and mountaineers surviving long periods in freezing cold. Their bodies shut down to save them—just like a form of hibernation.

Mystery File:
SNOW SURVIVAL

In 2011, Peter Skyllberg was trapped in his car by snow. Temperatures dropped to -22°F (-30°C). Huddled inside a sleeping bag, his body shut down. When he was found after two months he was near death, but miraculously was still alive.

Mystery words...

trance: a state of being awake but semiconscious

SLEEPWALKING

In 2009, a teenager in southern England fell 25 feet (7.6 meters) from her bedroom window to the ground below. She was completely uninjured. Doctors guessed that it was because she was relaxed during the accident—because she was fast asleep.

A sleepwalker has no idea what he or she is doing.

Mystery words...

unconscious: not aware or not done on purpose

Sleepwalkers move around as if they are awake. Some do odd things, such as paint or cook. In the past sleepwalking was believed to be mysterious. People thought that sleepwalkers were acting out their dreams. Later, people thought that sleepwalking was a sign that someone had unstable emotions.

Common Disorder

Today, doctors know that sleepwalking is an **unconscious** activity. It is quite common. Many children sleepwalk, but grow out of it.

Mystery File:
WAKE-UP CALL

It was once believed that waking a sleepwalker was dangerous. That's a myth. But waking a sleepwalker can cause a nasty shock--after all, they are not aware of what they are doing! It's best to guide them gently back to bed.

Walking on FIRE

On some islands in Polynesia and in parts of Asia, walking barefoot on red hot coals is an important way of marking the move into adulthood. But how do fire walkers avoid getting badly burned feet?

Ash on the coals helps to protect the soles of the feet.

In certain cultures, fire walking was a traditional display of courage. It also showed that a young person had learned to control pain. Some people say that fire walking is proof of "mind over matter." They claim that the human mind is so powerful that it can block pain and injury with the power of positive thought.

Corporate Training

The idea that fire walking is the result of a powerful mental attitude has made it popular among some companies. Fire walking can help train employees to be confident and positive.

Skeptics say that the mind has nothing to do with fire walking. They say that science makes it possible for anyone to walk on hot coals. Fire walkers always walk on hot coals, never on surfaces such as hot metal. Think of what happens to a hamburger when it is placed on a hot grill.

Fire walking is traditional on many islands in Polynesia.

Mystery File:
HOT COALS

The ability to fire walk comes down to insulation, poor conduction, and speed. The hot coals are almost pure carbon, which is a poor conductor of heat. They are covered in ash, which is a good insulator. And fire walkers usually walk quickly!

Mystery words...

skeptic: people who doubt the truth of an argument

Human
PINCUSHIONS

In Victorian times, a popular circus act involved a performer piercing his body with blades, like swords. Even though the blades broke the skin, they did not draw blood or leave permanent scars.

The practice of body piercing wasn't just a circus trick. It had a very long tradition. People pierced their bodies over 4,000 years ago in ancient India, China, and Egypt. In religions such as Hinduism, some worshipers push nails through their cheeks or tongues. Others push hooks into their skin. They use ropes tied to the hooks to pull weights or to be suspended in the air themselves. Such an act, shows that they are willing to suffer for their devotion.

On a bed of nails, a person's weight is spread out evenly.

Mystery words...

fakir: an Indian holy man

Piercing was also done for medical reasons. The Chinese practice of acupuncture involves sticking many small needles into the skin.

Dangerous Practice

Body piercing isn't magic. It can go very wrong. In 1947, **Fakir Mirin Dajo** had a thin sword pushed through his body. A year later, he died from a wound probably caused by the sword.

One form of body piercing is sword swallowing. A swallower spends years training his or her mouth, throat, and windpipe to relax. A blade can then go down into the stomach in a straight line.

This devoted Hindu man has pierced his skin with hooks.

Wild CHILDREN

Tarzan was said to have been raised in the jungle by apes.

In 1724, a "naked, brownish, black-haired" boy was captured in Germany. "Wild Peter" climbed trees, couldn't talk, and lived off plants. He was the first famous wild child.

Mystery words...

hoaxes: acts that deceive someone into believing what is not true

Some people believe that animals such as wolves can raise human children. The children are taught to behave like the animals. They sleep in the wild, make animal noises, and eat what animals eat.

Wild Sisters

In 1920, in India, two feral girls were caught. Kamala and Amala were scared of people and ate from bowls on the floor. It is believed that other children have survived in the wild by living like animals.

Do you think animals can raise human children? A lot of scientists are doubtful. They believe the cases of feral children are **hoaxes**.

Mystery File:
JUNGLE CHILDREN

One reason people are willing to believe in feral children may be the number of movies and books in which they are featured. The stories of Tarzan or Mowgli from *The Jungle Book*, make it seem very believable that a child could **survive** alone in the jungle.

Human MAGNETS

Can a mother in London, England, really make metal objects stick to her skin for 45 minutes? Brenda Allison says that tools, coins, and magnets stick to her and that electronic machines often malfunction near her.

All over the world, other individuals claim that metal objects stick to their skin. But how can human flesh have a magnetic field? One answer may lie in electricity. Our brains constantly emit tiny electrical pulses. They set up a weak magnetic field.

A human magnet can stick any metal object to his or her skin.

Humans have magnetic bones in their noses. Some scientists believe that these bones may be related to the ability to sense the Earth's magnetic field. Many different animals use a similar sense of magnetism to navigate.

Electromagnetism

The modern world has more **electromagnetic** fields than in the past because of the growth

Human magnets can be any age or sex, and exist around the world.

Mystery File: MAGNETIC POWERS

Animals and birds can detect magnetism. They use it to navigate and to hunt. A hammerhead shark hunts using the tiny electromagnetic field set up by its prey's gills. A homing pigeon uses Earth's magnetic field to find its way home.

in cell phone use and in WiFi Internet. Some people say this has increased the chances of a person becoming "magnetic."

Others say this is highly unlikely. They suggest that human magnets have more oils on their skin than other people. This oil allows objects to stick to their skin.

Mystery words...

electromagnetic: related to magnetism created by an electric current

Bionic BODIES

Bionic limbs can be controlled by the mind.

The hit 1970s' TV show "The Six Million Dollar Man" featured a man whose body was rebuilt with artificial parts. He had amazing strength. The show was fiction, but today **bionic** bodies are a reality.

Mystery words...

bionic: an artificial replacement for a human body part

Advances in medical science, with the help of computer technology, have allowed scientists to artificially reconstruct human body parts. Some parts of the body can already be replaced. A light-powered bionic eye can restore sight. Microchips send signals through the spinal cord to allow a person to move artificial limbs.

Future Breakthroughs

The next medical goal is to create organs, such as the liver. Today, livers must be transplanted from human donors. Artificial livers are still in the trial stage.

Extra Sensory
PERCEPTION

Does a dog really know when its owner is going to pull into the driveway? Do some people know what is going to happen before it happens? Can people communicate through thought alone?

Usually, we interpret the world around us by using physical senses, such as sight, smell, hearing, taste, and touch. Some people claim to have a "sixth sense"—extrasensory **perception** (ESP). The mind receives signals we cannot sense in any other way, such as the feeling that something bad is going to happen.

There are many stories, for example, of people who feel strange senses of dread that makes them cancel trips. They later learn the airplanes or trains they would have been on crashed. Their sixth sense saved them.

Alternative View

Skeptics say that such events are **coincidences**, not ESP. They say that an ESP experience is only understood through its interpretation. Many people dread particular events, for example, but nothing bad happens.

Mystery File: ABSENT EVIDENCE

People who don't believe in a sixth sense seek **rational** ways to explain events. They point out that a sense of fear might actually have been felt after a disaster, not before. Or that people don't remember their feelings accurately.

Mystery words...

rational: something that is supported by reason and evidence

Elastic BODIES

Imagine squeezing yourself into a small box. Not possible? It is for contortionists. They bend their limbs into impossible shapes to fit into tiny spaces. They would like you to believe that they have special powers, but do they?

Some tricks that contortionists do seem impossible. They fold themselves into containers the size of suitcases, or bend over backwards. It seems that their bodies are more elastic than everyone else's.

All human bodies are a little flexible, but contortionists are very, very flexible. Their bodies can bend into unusual positions that other people would find impossible.

Contortionists fit into tiny spaces without injury.

High flexibility

Some contortionists are born with extra flexible bodies. Others spend years training their bodies. Like gymnasts, contortionists have flexible spines that can bend either forward or backward. This allows them to squeeze into tiny spaces. Daniel Browning Smith holds a world record for squeezing through a tennis racquet and a toilet seat. The key is to spend a lot of time stretching and to learn the best sequence for getting into and out of small spaces.

Mystery File: DISLOCATION

Contortionists seem to be able to **dislocate** their joints. But making a joint come out of its socket is very painful. In fact, some super-flexible people can put their joints out without actually dislocating them.

Mystery words...

dislocate: to pull a joint in the body from its socket

27

Holding their BREATH

It is important to learn not to panic when you can not get oxygen.

If most people tried holding their breath, they might manage anything between a few seconds and a minute. In 2012, a new world record was set by someone who held their breath underwater for 22 minutes and 22 seconds.

A German named Tom Sietas set the record. He can hold his breath far longer than most people. Many people would have drowned. But there are no tricks. For centuries, pearl divers in Japan and islands in the Pacific Ocean have taught themselves to hold their breath for long periods of time. They spend many minutes on the seabed looking for pearls.

Special Preparation

Not everyone could achieve such a feat. It helps to have big lungs. Sietas' lung capacity is 20 percent bigger than normal. He also used a tank to fill his lungs with pure oxygen. Without the oxygen, his best time is 10 minutes, 12 seconds.

As with many feats, the most important thing is practice. The key is not to panic when the body starts longing for air.

Mystery File: DIVING REFLEX

It is easier to hold your breath in water than in air. In cold water, the diving reflex kicks in. It diverts blood from the rest of the body to the heart and brain. The body needs less oxygen, so can last longer without it.

Mystery words...

reflex: an automatic response to something

Glossary

adrenaline A chemical in the body that releases strength and helps overcome pain

bionic An artificial replacement for a human body part

circulation The system by which blood moves around the body

coincidence Events that occur at the same time, but are only related by accident

combustion Catching fire

conductor Something that transmits heat

contortionists People who can bend their body in unusual ways

devotion Dedication to a particular religious belief

dislocate To pull a joint from its socket

electromagnetic Magnetic fields created by an electric current

engulfed Completely covered

fakir An Indian holy man

feat A remarkable achievement

hoaxes Acts that deceive someone into believing something that is not true

insulator Something that stops or slows the flow of heat

meditation When a person focuses all their attention in their mind and completely relaxes the body

oddities Traits or features that are odd, strange, or unusual

perception Receiving signals from our surroundings and interpreting them

rational Something that is supported by reason and evidence

reflex an automatic response to something

skeptics People who doubt the truth of an argument

spontaneous Something that happens suddenly for no apparent reason

trance A state of being awake but semiconscious

unconscious Not aware or not done on purpose

Find Out More

BOOKS

Calkhoven, Laurie. *Fearless Feats* (Guinness World Records) Turtleback, 2006.

Stone, Adam. *ESP* (Torque Books: The Unexplained). Bellwether Media, 2010.

Impossible Feats (Ripley's Believe It Or Not...). Mason Crest, 2010.

Woog, Adam. *The Bionic Hand* (Great Ideas). Norwood House Press, 2009.

Nobleman, Marc Tyler. *Contortionists and Cannons: An Acrobatic Look at the Circus*, Heinemann Raintree, 2010.

WEBSITES

Remarkable feats
Livescience.com list of seven remarkable human feats.
www.livescience.com/14048-amazing-superhuman-feats.html

Adrenaline rush
Howstuffworks.com about the effects of adrenaline on the body.
http://entertainment.howstuffworks.com/arts/circus-arts/adrenaline-strength.htm

Feats of survival
BBC News article about great feats of endurance and survival.
www.bbc.co.uk/news/magazine-15129343

Index

acupuncture 17
animals 7, 9, 10, 18–19, 21
Atlas 6

bionics 22–23
Blade Runner 23
Bleak House 8
body piercing 16–17
breath, holding 28–29

children 13, 18–19
China 17
cold, extreme 11
contortionists 5, 26–27

Dickens, Charles 8
diving reflex 29

electricity 20
electromagnetism 20–21
emotions 13
extra sensory perception 24–25

feral children 18–19
fire walking 14–15
flexibility 26, 27

gymnasts 27

hibernation 10–11

Hinduism 16, 17
hysterical strength 7

India 9, 16, 17
insulation 11, 15

joints 27

limbs 23
lungs 29

magnets, human 20–21
medicine 22–23
mind over matter 14

navigation 21

organs 23

pain 4, 14
piercing 4, 16–17
pincushions, human 16–17
Pistorius, Oscar 23
Polynesia 14, 15
premonitions 25

science 15
senses 24
Sietas, Tom 29
sixth sense 24, 25
sleepwalking 12–13
Smith, Daniel Browning 27

spontaneous human combustion 5, 8–9
strength 6–7
survival 11
sword-swallowing 17

Tarzan 18, 19

unconscious 13

weightlifting 6, 7
whales 9
wick effect 9
wild children 18–19

yogis 9–10